S0-BNV-929

Sock on the LOOSE

Conor McGlauflin

Roaring Brook Press

New York

Socks come in twos,
snuggled up in your shoes.

They give your feet cuddles
when you splash in puddles.

And they warm your small toes
whenever it snows.

Once back inside,
it's time to get dry.

They go for a wash,

then for a spin.

Now off to bed,
tucked in with its twin.

At night they sleep tight,
matching pairs in a row.

Until—wait a minute! Oh no!
Where did other Blue Sock go?

Did it run away with a moose?

Sneak off for some juice?

Whatever happened,

it's a . . .

SOCK ON THE

LOOSE!

Perhaps just like you,
it has things it must do!

Or maybe this sock wants to explore
the great big world outside of its drawer.

So it's off to a place where nothing is stinky.
No heels, no toes, and no little pinkies.

No pairs, no matching—just freedom and fun.

No wonder this little sock's on the run!

And look, it's not the only one!

Fuzzy Sock wants to polka with Dot.
Old Sock learns how to tie a bowknot.

Sport Sock finds a new pair of heels.
Striped Sock splashes around
with some seals.

There are so many things a sock can do
when given the chance to try something new.

Surf a big moon wave!
Explore a watermelon cave!

Try a new look!
Learn how to cook!

After days of fun and lots of adventure,
Blue Sock is sleepy and starts to remember—

its friends in rows, so tidy and neat,
and the comfort of snuggling your little feet.

It seems Blue Sock
is not on its own.

Some of its friends
also want to go home!

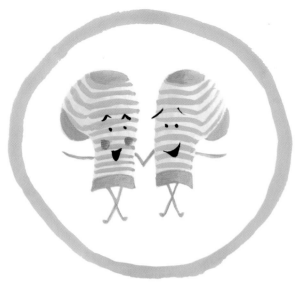

Striped Sock misses
its other half.

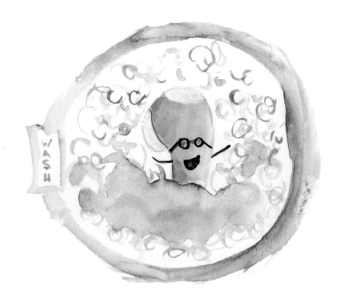

Old Sock needs
a hot bubble bath.

Sport Sock wants
a sneaker sole.

Fuzzy Sock feels like
a nice, long stroll.

You see, a sock on the loose
has been known to come back.

So don't lose hope
if you can't keep track.

Through the door and over the floor,
Blue Sock might return while you snore.

So the next time a sock
is not on its shelf,

don't worry . . .

It's just finding itself!

To Hannah,
whose love and support
brought this story to life